CELESTIAL
FALLS

Aurora's Fae Prince

LONI REE

AURORA'S FAE PRINCE

Edited By: Kendra's Editing and Book Services

Cover Design By: Cormar Covers

✺ Created with Vellum

Author's Note

Please note this story was previously published as *His Curvy Goddess by Loni Ree* in the Wolves & Warriors Anthology.

The story has been updated and re-edited. The overall outcome of the story remains the same.

PROLOGUE - VALENTINO AMOR (CUPID)

Many years ago, life changed for every "Eternal." Romulus and Remus, my dumbass stepbrothers, brought about the great reveal by accident. To add insult to injury, it was all because of a female. A mortal woman, to be exact. During the past twelve millennia, the two hotheads had been butting heads. It all came to a head when the two immortal gods lost their minds and threw a hissy fit in public.

We had been living hidden among our human neighbors since the dawn of time. Blending in was easy until modern technology came along and changed everything. Everyone has a cellular phone with a high-tech camera. And that little feature bit us in the ass. During their argument, the two hotheads lost control. Their roars shattered windows for blocks before they progressed to throwing lightning bolts at each other's heads.

The entire downtown area stopped to watch the show, and quite a few mortals recorded it. Within minutes, the videos spread throughout social media and *boom*. We were out of the paranormal closet. The Eternal Parliament had no choice but to announce our existence and hope for the best.

Shock, fear, and turmoil followed for the next two years while we worked hard to convince humans that we don't present a threat to their survival. Their long-held beliefs about "monsters" began to change over time, and humans slowly accepted our kind. We stopped hiding in the shadows, and most mortals either ignore our existence or embrace it. For some crazy human women, bedding an Eternal has become the new status symbol.

Nearly all supernatural beings have a preordained true mate, and no one else will ever satisfy them. Since the dawn of time, many beings have struggled to find the other half of their soul.

The Fates have a perverse sense of humor. The three old biddies love throwing obstacles in the paths of everlasting happiness for both Eternals and humans just to watch the fireworks. Eons ago, these juvenile tricks irritated the Goddess of Love, my mother. She created me to help counterbalance the meddling old ladies.

Silly fairytales claim I run around in a diaper shooting arrows at unsuspecting individuals, and *boom*, there's an instant love connection. I wish. Blending in requires dressing in human attire, and my celestial bow shoots invisible, golden threads that tie the lovebirds together for all eternity.

Stubborn, pain-in-the-ass Eternals make my job a nightmare when they fight the attraction. It's a losing battle for them. You can't outrun your destiny. Whether human or paranormal, no one except their true love will ever truly satisfy them. However, free will allows mortals to fight the connection, and they often ignore the feelings The Fates have created. When this happens, they end up with a completely incompatible mate.

My demanding bosses deliver their commands to me, and I get to work. Before I start the whole process, I must ensure the two love birds are ready for what's coming. After arranging the first meeting between soulmates, I meddle a little and then stand back while the mate bond does the rest.

At least, that's how it is supposed to work. Unfortunately, things don't fall into place every time.

Ten years after the big revelation, I learned this lesson and almost lost my own soulmate in the process. The Fates don't take too kindly to romance fuck-ups, and I pulled the mother of all oopsies. In my defense, the whole mating was a clusterfuck, but that didn't matter to my bitchy bosses.

Wolves are beasts to match. No pun intended. The uncouth fuckers are all "I'm going to bite you and keep you." Once they mark their mate, the bond is sealed for all eternity. One tiny slip-up by me—my arrow hitting the wrong toothy motherfucker— was the end of the fucking world. When the wrong wolf ended up sinking his teeth into his twin brother's predestined mate, my bosses were pissed off. Supremely. In my defense, a little witch's spell started the whole trainwreck heading down the tracks.

Stormy Loinnir got wind of my upcoming match for her and the surly wolf and decided to take matters into her own hands. The witch's interference caused my golden threads to wrap around the wrong twin brother. My bad. I shudder remembering my horror when I discovered my mistake. It took a while, but I managed to arrange mate bonds for both Blackthorne twins. It all worked out in the end for everyone involved, but we had a bumpy ride getting there.

My crabby bosses have forgiven me, and life is good. Or so I thought. Evidently, messing with my own mating wasn't enough to satisfy them. They're turning their attention to my children.

AURORA

"I cannot believe this!" I slam my hand down on my mother's desk. "I don't want to decorate the big jerk's house." I'd rather have toothpicks run under my fingernails.

My mother sits back in her chair, shaking her head. "Now, Aurora." I wince at her chastising tone, preparing myself for the speech I know is coming.

"We can't turn down opportunities because you don't like the clients." She tsks me and I feel like a teenager again. I wish she'd send me to my room without dinner instead of making me deal with the biggest jerk in the universe.

"You've dealt with difficult clients before," she reminds me. "Remember your grandmother's custom kitchen."

Yuck. Do I ever. Try making the Goddess of Love happy. It's impossible. My eccentric family doesn't do moderation. When your mother is a cougar shifter and your dad is Cupid, the real Cupid, the freaking God of Love, you live an unusual existence. Shifters, gods, supernatural beings. It's all in a day's work for Cupid.

My parents own the supernatural matchmaking agency, Whiskers & Wings Matchmaking. They are responsible for nearly all the matches between Eternals and their intended mates. Over the years, I've become numb to the whole romance scene that surrounds my famous father.

To get away from everything hearts and kisses related, I chose to pursue my mother's former career, Interior Design. After college, I couldn't find a position that fit me and decided to open my own company with my inheritance. My mother jumped on board and became my partner. She works two days a week at Whiskers & Wings and the other three days at Design Goddesses.

My older brother, August, graduated with a computer engineering degree and hides away in his apartment working on his computers. Neither of us expects our overprotective father to find true love for us.

My mother snaps her fingers in front of my face, bringing me back to the conversation. "I mean, Nix Dixon dropped off the radar several years ago. Maybe he's changed since the last time you saw him."

I freaking doubt it. A lobotomy wouldn't cure the big jerk of his cold, condescending attitude. Nix's father, a great fae commander, met and fell in love with a beautiful dragon.

Over time, Oberon Dixon began to cut back on his work duties as their marriage changed the cold, calculating fae into a pussycat. The General ended up retiring from his high-stress job to spend more time with his lovely wife.

The younger fae desired his father's position but wasn't a great candidate. He had to prove to the fae rulers he could change. It took several years, but Nix managed to transform from the careless, reckless, irresponsible jerk into a cold, calculating general.

My dad sounds a little jealous when he talks about Oberon Dixon retiring "to play golf and goof off," but he knows the Fates aren't going to let Cupid quit making matches any time soon.

Growing up with the God of Love as your father tends to sour your perception of the emotion. I mean, what part of love is real, and what comes from my father's interference? Maybe I should join a convent? Then I'd have a valid excuse to avoid this meeting.

All night long, I toss and turn, worrying about my upcoming meeting with Nix Dixon. The last time I saw the handsome fae, he whizzed into my eighteenth birthday party and crushed my vulnerable heart by insulting me and my party. I can still picture the pinched, incensed look on his face when he roared, "Who let her wear that dress? Her tits and ass are on display."

My father and Blaze Fier, the fierce dragon CEO and Nix's stepbrother, pulled the irate fae from the room. The two men returned a while later minus the fae, and no one ever mentioned the whole humiliating experience again.

The party went on as if my teenage heart wasn't shattered. I'd worn the slinky, figure-hugging dress to attract Nix's attention and boy did I ever regret it. After the party, I avoided the jerk like the plague. That worked great for five years. Now, through some trick of fate, he'll be my only client for the foreseeable future. Fudge my life.

Maybe the fae commander will be so busy that I barely ever lay eyes on him. Not likely, but a girl can wish.

After my restless night, it takes a little extra concealer to hide the purple circles under my eyes. I dress in my most conservative suit and pull my curly, blonde hair up into a bun. That should prove to him that I'm all business.

CHAPTER 2

NIX

Fuck, she's gorgeous. "Hello." I hold out my hand, sounding like a fucking moron. "It's good to see you again." That's a goddamn understatement. The last time I laid eyes on Cupid's daughter, she was a stunning, curvy, way-the-fuck too young goddess. Trying to ignore the intense feelings running through my soul, I made a total jackass out of myself and sent my little soulmate into hiding. Knowing I hurt her kills me, but it was necessary. She needed time to grow up, and I still had to prove myself worthy of Cupid's daughter.

"You, too." Sparks shoot through my body, lighting it up from the inside out when her soft palm touches mine. Aurora smiles, but her expressive green eyes tell me it's a show. She'd rather be anywhere but here with me, and I honestly can't blame her. I have my work cut out for me if I want to convince the goddess who owns my heart to forgive me, but I'll do whatever it takes to make her mine. Even take on the God of Love.

"Would you like to have a seat, and we can discuss business?" I point at the chrome and leather torture device in front of my desk and wince. This is why I need to have my home remodeled. The over-the-top tacky decor Arond, my former assistant, chose has suddenly gotten old. As a fae commander, I'm rarely on the Celestial Falls side of the Olympian Barrier, the portal that separates the human-shifter world from our fae realm. Figuring I would never be here, I allowed my eccentric former assistant to have free rein when renovating the apartment. Big fucking mistake. I can't take this atrocity any longer.

When my dragon stepmother suggested I hire Design Goddesses to redecorate my penthouse, I saw the advantages. I get Aurora alone in my home for the foreseeable future, and my soulmate will decorate the apartment to meet her tastes.

"Thank you." She's stiff as a board. I watch the curvy little cougar-goddess slide into the uncomfortable chair before walking around my desk to sit in my own torture device. "I want to apologize in advance. My mother took the information from your assistant." She gets right down to business. "So, I only have the bare basics. You want your entire penthouse remodeled?" She raises an eyebrow, waiting for me.

Her choice of words brings to mind fantasies of her delicious, curvy body spread out bare-ass naked on my black silk sheets. Slamming the door on my inconveniently timed thoughts, I pull myself together and smile. "Let's take a walk through the apartment and I'll show you the problem." A picture is worth a thousand words. She can see the train wreck for herself.

I listen to her high heels click on the marble floors as she follows me through the penthouse. My cock grows hard at the thought of those heels digging into my back as I fuck her into next year. I pull my jacket closed to hide the evidence of what my little goddess does to me and concentrate on the job at hand. Winning my soulmate's heart.

Stopping every now and then, I point out horrendously awful parts. "I want that monstrosity gone," I growl. Who in the hell puts a naked cherub smoking a cigar standing over a large oval bathtub? I shudder internally, wondering if my former assistant had mental issues. Maybe I'll donate the horrible artwork to Aurora's father.

"We can definitely get rid of that." As Aurora's lips twitch, I feel my cock harden even further. The fucker is imagining those juicy lips are coming for him. In my mind, I can picture her kneeling in front of me sucking my cock to the back of her throat. The fantasies are getting too real. Pulling my head out of my ass, I give her a forced smile and continue the tour before I throw her down on the bed and demonstrate my fantasies.

"Why don't we have lunch and discuss the specifics?" I lay my palm across her back and feel electricity slide up my spine. Fuck. I'm in so much trouble. At this moment, I can see why Cupid lets his wife carry his balls around in her purse. These Amor women pack a punch.

My phone buzzes in my pocket, interrupting our meeting, and I intend to ignore it until I hear my stepbrother's voice in my head. "Pick up, asshole." Fucker. I hate that the dragon bastard can pull the annoying little trick.

"Excuse me." I lead Aurora into the living room. "I have to take a call."

Rushing to my office, I close the door and pull out my blasted cellphone. Glancing down, I see four missed calls from my stepbrother. "What the fuck do you want?" That asshole hasn't ever reached out to me this many times in one day.

"I'm trying to help you," Blaze growls. "My mother begged me to make sure you don't fuck up things with Aurora."

Why does my entire family think I'm going to fuck this up? "I don't need your help." I pinch the bridge of my nose, trying to thwart the massive headache beginning in my temples.

"I beg to differ." In my mind, I picture the arrogant asshole shaking his head. "You fucked it up royally the last time." The horrified look on eighteen-year-old Aurora's beautiful face flashes through my mind causing my heart to clench. I might've fucked things up with her years ago, but I won't make the same mistake again.

"I'll call you if I need help." I hang up the phone, knowing it will be a cold day in hell before I ask the asshole for assistance. After taking a deep breath to calm my nerves, I return to my curvy goddess. It's time to pull out all the stops to win the beauty who bowled me over all those years ago.

CHAPTER 3
AURORA

By the time he returns, I've managed to come up with a plausible excuse to avoid having lunch with him. I already know working with the fae commander is going to be a nightmare. I don't want to spend any extra time with him if I can help it.

"Sorry about that." Standing at the window with my back to him, I feel him step closer, and a shiver runs through me as he explains, "I'd been waiting on that call for a while."

"No problem." Drawing in a deep breath, I turn to Nix. "I'm afraid I'll have to take a rain check on lunch." Hopefully, my red cheeks don't scream I'm lying through my teeth. "I forgot all about an important meeting in town."

He stares at me for a few moments, and I squirm under his perusal. "I'm disappointed," Nix finally concedes. The heat shining in his intense ice blue eyes sends goosebumps racing up my spine. "Maybe another time?"

No way in hell. "I'll get some ideas put together and an estimate drawn up and email it to you within a few days?" I offer him as professionally as my mushy mind allows. I need to get home and shore up my defenses. Falling at the big jerk's feet is totally unacceptable.

He stares at me for a few seconds, and I'm scared he's going to give me a hard time but the fae commander surprises me. "That sounds great." He smiles and places his hand gently on my back to walk me to the door. The heat from his touch causes very dirty thoughts to take over my mind.

"I'll have my assistant send you a set of keys and the passcode for the entrance."

Great. Just what I need. Easy access to the man who makes my pulse race and my panties wet. What could possibly go wrong in this scenario?

For the next two days, I manage to avoid my new employer by working on his project. My mother frowns and rolls her eyes when I dance around the office, celebrating my success in receiving the apartment dimensions from Nix's assistant. Now, I can work on ideas and pricing for at least two more days.

"You're going to have to face him." My mother stares at me, and I suddenly feel like I'm fifteen again.

"I know." I shrug, reminding myself I just need a few days to strengthen my defenses against the big jerk. I breathe a sigh of relief when she leaves early to meet my dad for a date night.

Sleepless nights are catching up with me, and I'm turning into a grouch. Every time I close my eyes, Nix appears in my dreams. It's freaky how vivid the fantasies are. I swear I feel his warm breath brushing against my ear as he whispers all the dirty things he's planning to do to me. Each morning, I wake up tired, horny, and ready to scream my frustration.

First thing Friday morning, I email Nix my ideas and a rough estimate. Within fifteen minutes, I receive approval from him. What? There's no way he could've gone through all fifteen attachments. Surely, this is a mistake. I grab my cellphone and dial his number.

"Good morning." His deep voice with the English accent wakes up my hunger. "I was just about to call you."

"Hi," I manage to squeak out. "I wanted to talk to you about your email."

"Great," he agrees. "Let's meet for breakfast at the Shooting Star Café, and we can discuss it."

Woah. I wasn't expecting to see Nix today. I thought I'd have at least the weekend to prepare. "Okay," slips out of my mouth before I'm able to stop it. We arrange to meet in an hour and hang up.

I glance down at my outfit and groan. Of course, he'd want to meet on the day I wear sweats and a t-shirt to the office. In my defense, I work in my basement, so it's not like anyone except my mother sees me most days.

I rush upstairs praying for a minor miracle. Glancing in the mirror, I groan at my reflection. I'll need divine intervention to fix my dark circles and messy hair. Twenty minutes later, I stare in the mirror after applying lip gloss. Satisfied with my transformation, I send a quick thanks to my grandmother. It's kinda nice having the Goddess of Love looking out for you. She listened to my pleas and gave me a little magical bump. Now, I have just enough time to dress and head to the café. After digging through my packed closet, I finally decide to wear a black suit and pale pink blouse. Time to pull up my big girl panties and head out.

Before rushing out the door, I leave a note for my mother. She'll have a cow if she finds my house empty when she arrives.

CHAPTER 4
NIX

Years ago, I was an immature, moronic, asshole fae prince flitting my way through my existence. My wake-up call came when my father decided to retire. He recommended another fae to replace him on the war council. The horror of being bypassed for the appointment brought me to my senses, but it was too late. I was forced to prove myself worthy before the fae high rulers would consider allowing me to assume my family's honored position.

Bad timing brought my soulmate into my life while I was still fighting for my position in the fae world. Knowing I needed to accomplish my goals before approaching Aurora, I acted like a jackass. My stunt sent my little goddess running, and I spent the next several years missing her. Proving myself worthy of both the commander position and as Aurora's mate was my only goal. Once I achieved my objective, the invisible barrier holding back our mating disappeared.

Vivid, steamy dreams started the night of our meeting as my body urges me to cement the bond with my mate. My heart and soul belong to the curvy little goddess, and there's no way to hold back the floodgates any longer.

The invisible band tethering us steadily grows stronger every second. Within another week or so, our life forces will be completely intertwined. That gives me about seven days to prove to my sassy little goddess that the Fates haven't screwed the pooch. We are meant to be.

I'm sitting at a small booth in the back of the Shooting Star Café when I sense Aurora. Shit. The bond is growing fast, much quicker than I expected. I watch her move through the crowded restaurant and growl when I notice several other fuckers staring at my girl, too. My lips twitch with the urge to kiss the vein pulsing on the side of her elegant throat.

I barely resist throwing my curvy goddess over my shoulder and running for the nearest exit. But my reasonable side knows I have my work cut out for me. I have to convince Cupid's daughter that we're soulmates while keeping her father out of our business.

It would be a shame to start a supernatural war over our mating, but I won't let anything stand in my way. Aurora Amor is mine.

Her sweet scent floats around me, instantly turning my cock to stone. Ignoring the fucker, I pull her close to place a soft kiss on her cheek. "You look beautiful," I whisper under her ear and watch goosebumps erupt on her delicate skin.

"Thank you." She bites her plump bottom lip and smiles shyly. Fuck, this girl is turning me into a raving madman. One little smile, and Aurora has me wrapped around her finger.

She slides into the booth, and I sit close to my mate. The young waiter comes by for our orders, and I glare at the little shit, warning him to keep his eyes off of her. While we wait for our breakfast, Aurora jumps into discussing the design job.

"Did you have a chance to go through the proposal?" she asks before wrapping her luscious lips around her straw. As she drinks, images of those lips sucking on my hard rod overtake my thoughts. Swallowing, I attempt to drag my mind out of the gutter, but it's nearly impossible with my curvy girl sitting next to me.

"Huh?" Great. I sound like a fucking moron. Clearing my throat, I try again. "Yes. I looked over everything, and I'm ready to get started." On the apartment and cementing our relationship.

"Do you have any questions for me?" She smiles at me, and my mind empties of all thoughts.

"When can you start?"

Aurora blinks several times before shrugging. "Monday?"

"Perfect," I agree. That gives me three days to get ready for my campaign. My wooing campaign. The most important fight of my life.

I listen to her soft voice explain that next week will be measuring and ordering materials. The real work won't begin for at least two more weeks.

"I understand." By then, I plan to have her tied to me for life. "Why don't you move into my guest quarters?" The brilliant idea pops into my mind and I run with it. "That way you're always around to handle anything that crops up." Before Aurora can reject my offer, I rush on. "I have a guest suite with a private entrance." My curvy goddess' eyes widen, and I can tell she's frantically searching her brain for an excuse to refuse. "I spend a good portion of my time in Celestial Landing," I assure her. "You will barely ever see me." That might be a little fib.

Although my position on the Celestial Landing Council, our governing body, keeps me busy, I'm cutting back my hours. Once I decided my soulmate was ready for our bond, I informed the council of my intention to retire. My superiors asked me to train my replacement, and I agreed to remain in my position for a celestial quarter, six months in human terms. I'm midway through my retirement period.

The Fae realm, Celestial Landing, only allows fae born and their mates to cross into the Celestial

Barrier. Over the years, I've come to realize how much my mate's family means to her. Since moving to fae lands with me would require Aurora to leave her family behind for long stretches of time, there's no way I can ask her to make the sacrifice. It's too early to let her in on my plans to retire and move to the human side permanently. Once I win her over, I'll explain everything.

"I'll pack my things and bring them with me Monday morning." I blink several times, wondering if I heard Aurora correctly. My sassy little goddess just agreed without a fight. There is no way to predict her moves. This woman is going to keep me on my toes.

AURORA

I can't believe I agreed to live in his penthouse. Have I completely lost my mind? After our breakfast meeting, I return to my little house and find my mother sitting at her desk. "How did breakfast go?" she asks as I drop into my chair.

"Great." I sigh before explaining my meeting with Nix. Well, not everything. I leave out the part about me drooling over the gorgeous fae commander. "I start on Monday." That gives me two days to figure out how to tell my overprotective father I'm moving in with our client. Oops.

"Spit it out." My perceptive mother rolls her eyes, and I realize there is no keeping a secret from her.

"Nix asked me to stay in his guest quarters so I'm on hand to take care of any issues." That sounds weak but I run with it.

"I think that's a good idea." My mother surprises the heck out of me. "Nix Dixon is a very important client." Huh? I'll never understand my parents.

We spend the rest of the day going over all the estimates, ensuring I haven't missed anything. That evening, I drink a bottle of wine trying to quieten my crazy thoughts. The insane amount of alcohol buzzing through my veins allows me to sleep without dirty dreams for the first night since meeting Nix again. I wake up groggy, hungover, and disappointed in myself. I need to find another way of dealing with this situation.

Saturday afternoon, I'm busily packing my clothes when my doorbell rings. Pulling the door open, I blink several times when I find my father standing on my doorstep. "Daddy?" My parents spend every weekend together. It's shocking for him to show up alone. "Is everything okay?" I instantly worry something bad has happened.

"I don't want you staying at Nix Dixon's home." Oh. Great my mom threw me under the bus. He steps into my front hall and begins to pace. "I just need time." My usually unflappable father runs his hand through his messy hair. I can't remember the last time I saw him so disheveled. "To get the Fates to change their minds." He stares at me, waiting for me to understand this crazy conversation.

"Uh." I close the door and head for the kitchen. "Let me get you some lemonade, and we can talk." As I pour our drinks, his words run through my mind on a continuous loop. It hits me out of the blue that he mentioned the Fates, his three crabby bosses and the goddesses responsible for all paranormal mating. Oh, heck. Does that mean the

Fates have chosen a mate for me? Everything suddenly becomes crystal clear. Nix, the crazy dreams—all of it makes sense now. I'm in a lot of trouble.

I set his drink on the counter in front of him before sitting next to him. "Please, explain it to me."

"The Fates are still after me." He sighs. "They chose the asshole fae for you to get back at me."

My eyes widen as his words sink into my muddled mind. Holy cow. "Does Nix know?"

"I have no idea if the little shit has figured it out," my father groans. "I'm going to get this reversed." He slams his hand down on the counter. "There's no way my little girl is mating a conceited fae asshole. I won't let him take you to Celestial Landing."

I've heard stories about the fae realm that exists on the other side of the Olympian Barrier but never thought I'd ever see it. If my chosen mate is a fae, do I have to abandon my family and follow him there? My heart drops at the thought of leaving my family behind, but I also can't imagine living without Nix. Holy Cow. I almost pass out when I realize how much he already means to me. This is bad. So bad.

Standing in the hallway outside Nix's penthouse Monday morning, I wonder if I should run for the hills. He pulls the door open before I'm able to force my feet to move. "Hi." I smile at him, realizing there's no way to fight this. Time to embrace the craziness.

"Good morning, love." He leans over and places a soft kiss on my cheek, sending hunger shooting through my body. I manage to control my urges while he shows me the guest suite. "I'll have your bags brought up," he assures me. "Then we can get to work." Somehow, the handsome fae makes the words sound so intimate. Or is that my wishful thinking?

Nix shows me the desk he had set up for me in his office. I'm not sure I'll be able to concentrate in the same room with him, but I don't complain. Surprisingly, the first day actually goes by really fast and fairly smoothly.

The sun is setting when we give up for the day. "I've ordered dinner. It will be here in an hour." Nix closes his computer and pushes back from his desk. "Why don't you take a little break and freshen up?" That sounds heavenly.

A few minutes away from the powerful chemistry surrounding us will help me get my overheated body under control. Standing beneath the cold shower spray does absolutely nothing to cool the steamy fantasies running through my mind. I take my time getting ready, putting off the inevitable as long as possible.

I'm applying lip gloss when Nix knocks on my door. "Dinner is here."

Swallowing, I grab my cellphone and head out. Holy wow. He showered, too. The light glistens off his damp, white-blond hair. Dirty images of him standing naked under the cool water bombard my mind, heating my blood. I stare into his ice-blue eyes and see hunger shining back at me. I suddenly realize there's no fighting this mating. I mentally pull up my big girl panties. If the hot fae isn't going to make the first move, I guess I'll have to.

"Thank you for ordering dinner." His masculine scent wraps around me as he scoots my chair forward.

"My pleasure," he whispers next to my ear. Hunger of a different kind hits me.

I somehow manage to make it through the longest dinner in the history of eating without self-combusting. We discuss the plans for the penthouse, ignoring the chemistry swirling around us.

After pushing the food around on my plate for what seems like an eternity, I take a deep breath and blurt out, "Fighting this pull between us sucks." What the hell? My mouth just took off without consulting my brain.

"I don't plan on even trying anymore," Nix admits and stands to hold out his hand to me. "Let's talk." He leads me to the living room and points at the sofa. "I think it's time we lay our cards on the table."

It looks this is my opportunity to strike.

Staring into her emerald green eyes, I take a deep breath and explain, "I can't fight the pull to you any longer." The whole truth comes spilling out, and I don't hold anything back. "The night of your birthday party, I had a sudden, irrefutable realization. You're my mate, and I wouldn't change that for the world." Her eyes widen until they appear ready to pop from her gorgeous face. "The timing couldn't have been worse, though. I was fighting to prove myself to the fae council, and you were barely an adult. Our eternal future was too important to rush." I sit next to her and feel her luscious thigh brush against mine. The tiny touch sends unimaginable hunger blasting through my body, and my cock turns to stone. I ignore the discomfort and continue. "I'm sorry my inconsiderate words hurt you. My only regret was the way I treated you that night." Invisible fingers slide along my spine as I imagine my mate touching me.

Aurora opens and shuts her mouth several times. "Uh." She doesn't pull away when I reach for her soft hand. "I'm overwhelmed," my mate admits. "This is all so sudden and," she looks up at me and shrugs, "crazy."

"I'm ready to embrace the craziness." I run my finger over the vein pounding at the base of her neck. "Are you?"

"I thought you'd never ask." She wraps her soft hand around the back of my head and pulls me down for her kiss.

Fuck. I nearly come in my pants as her tongue slides against mine. I pull her luscious curves close and slip my hand under her shirt. Sparks ignite as I touch her soft skin.

I need to feel every inch of her curvy body. As her luscious lips move against mine, my cock grows steadily harder. Aurora reaches between us and touches my erection. I suddenly want all the material to disappear. When her soft hand wraps around my cock, I realize my fae magic listened to my command. She pulls back, and I watch her eyes move over my naked body. "Nice trick." She swallows and stares intently at my rapidly expanding member. The heat of her touch burns me from the inside out.

"Can you do that for me, too?" She raises an eyebrow while glancing down at her black slacks and soft white sweater.

My future with Aurora is too important to fuck up, so I pull back. "Are you sure this is what you want?" I ask, knowing I'll never let her get away. I might be able to slow things down if she needs time, but the mate bond is too strong to completely resist.

She digs her sharp little nails into my scalp before running her tongue along my collarbone. "Please make my clothes disintegrate and fuck me."

She doesn't have to ask me twice. After snapping my fingers, I lift her luscious, naked body into my arms and head for her suite. I refuse to make love to my soulmate in my hideously decorated bedroom. I place kisses on the soft skin under her ear and whisper, "I won't ever let you go." She needs to know what giving herself to me means.

After laying her across the bed, I drop to my knees and spread her curvy thighs. Her taste hits me right between the eyes as I devour my mate's juicy pussy.

Her perfect tits bounce as she arches her back. I watch a shiver run through her stunning body when I slide my finger deep into her tightness. "Uh." She gives my hair a little tug. "Is it too late to tell you I've never done this?" My cock leaks cum onto the marble floor at the thought of fucking her virgin pussy. I rub her silky inner walls while nibbling on her clit. Her back arches when she comes screaming my name. I wait for the little flutters to stop before kissing my way up her soft body.

Staring into her worried eyes, I admit, "Neither have I." It's not unusual for paranormal beings to wait for their intended mates. "We'll figure it out together." And with a little help from my fae magic.

"There's no way that is going to fit there." She points down to her bare cunt. "Unless you use a little magic."

"Don't worry, love. There's nothing little about my magic." I wink at her. I suck her pebble-hard nipple into my mouth and run my tongue around the tight bud. "We will fit together perfectly," I promise her.

"I really like your magic wand." She wraps her silky hand around my cock and slides her thumb over the wetness leaking from the tip. "I hope to use it quite a bit in the future." She wiggles her eyebrows.

AURORA

I trust my mate and his magic wand to make it work. Staring into his ice-blue eyes, I force myself to relax. His hard cock jerks in my grasp, causing hunger to flow through my veins. All my concerns disappear as he leans forward and runs his tongue around my nipple.

"Please," I beg and watch his eyes flash red as I pump my hand.

"Anything for my little love." His hardness presses against my opening, and I force my inner muscles to relax. My mind shuts down as Nix slowly pushes into my inexperienced pussy.

My back arches as pleasure overwhelms me. He thrusts deep, and I feel every inch of his huge cock rubbing against my pussy walls.

"I fucking love you," he hisses. Intense pleasure overshadows the tiny sting as I dig my heels into the soft bedding and raise my hips to meet his. My nails dig into his muscular sides while I hold on for the ride. His grunts mix into one long growl, "My mate." Instinctively, I open my mind to his and feel our thoughts combine.

"I love you, too," I cry out. The words have been hiding in the back of my subconsciousness since my eighteenth birthday. Nix reaches between us to press on my clit, and I come unglued. His movements grow erratic before he suddenly freezes above me. Warmth fills my core, and I watch golden threads tie us together for eternity behind my closed eyelids. Tiny sparks continue to sizzle up my spine long after he drops to the bed and pulls me close.

The sun peeks through the heavy blinds, and I stretch, waking up from the best dream ever. My eyes pop open as the strong masculine arm wrapped around me tightens.

"Good morning, love," he whispers before kissing the side of my neck. I feel the heat of his body pressing against my back, and hunger flashes through my mind.

Too bad, my sore lady bits won't allow me to do anything about that. "Let's shower, then we'll have breakfast," Nix suggests in my mind. It's going to take some time to get used to having him share my thoughts.

"I'll teach you to control it." He smirks and lifts me into his arms. "I plan to make sure you're well-educated." He wiggles his eyebrows, and I roll my eyes at his silliness. It's shocking to see the cold, calculating fae commander acting carefree. "You'll get used to that, too." Darn bonded communication.

After we shower together, we head down to the kitchen to fix breakfast. "Fuck me," Nix growls, and I look over to see him frowning at the front door. "We're about to have company." He reaches for me. "I won't let your asshole father come between us."

What? Loud knocking on the front door interrupts our conversation. "Stay here," Nix orders me before heading to answer the door.

I squeak when I see my father punch my mate in the face. "I'll kill you, asshole," my dad roars and jumps on him. Nix deflects my father's swings but doesn't hit him back.

"Stop!" I shout, trying to stop them. "Daddy, if you hit my mate one more time, I will never talk to you again." My warning causes both men to still.

"Your mate?" My dad staggers over to the sofa, wheezing, "I'm too late?"

I roll my eyes and walk over to sit next to my dad. He knows eternal bonds can't be broken. "Nix is my mate." He opens his mouth, but I rush on before he can interrupt me. "I love him, and I won't let you interfere with our relationship."

There's another knock at the front door, and Nix walks over to answer it. "Oh my goodness." My mother takes in the scene. A tacky antique chair lies on its side next to a crushed end table. "I told you to calm down before rushing over here." She shakes her finger at my dad, and I barely hold back my laughter.

"I'm too late." My dad looks at her and sighs.

"Dramatic much?" She folds her arms in front of her chest and glares down at my dad. Out of the corner of my eye, I notice Nix running his hand over his face, trying to hide his smile.

My dad stands and glares at Nix. "You see?" He points to my mother. "This is what you have to look forward to. Pussy-whipped for life."

"I wouldn't change a thing." Nix walks over and stares at my parents. "Aurora is my mate, and there isn't anything you can do about it. I'd prefer if we discuss this like adults, but I have no problem throwing you out if you try to separate me from my mate."

"I'll shove my fist down your fucking throat," my father roars.

I'm about to argue my case when my mother turns to him. "Stop the freaking He-Man show. Now." My dad opens his mouth and pauses.

"She's my only daughter." His shoulders sag.

"And she's in love." My mother pats his leg. "Aurora is still our daughter. Now, shut up and let's get to know her mate."

CHAPTER 8

NIX

The God of Love glares at me but doesn't take another swing at me. At least the asshole listens to his wife. For a second there, I thought I might have to throw my mate's father out and kidnap her.

"Please, sit down."

Aurora's mother smiles at me, and I see where my girl got her beauty. The cougar shifter doesn't look a day older than twenty-five. I know she helps run two companies all while keeping her asshole husband in line. "Call me Layla." She points her thumb at the seething god sitting next to her. "And you can call my husband Val," she insists, causing Cupid to sputter.

"Would you like something to drink?" My fae grandmother would have my ass if I didn't offer my guests refreshments. When my mate's parents both refuse, I sit in the overstuffed chair across from them.

Layla Amor takes over the conversation like a pro. The tension hanging heavy in the air slowly dissipates as we talk.

"Do you plan to take my daughter to Celestial Landing and trap her there? Away from her family?" Cupid glares at me, and I notice the heat of his stare has lessened.

"No." I walk over and take Aurora's hand in mine. "I'm retiring from the war council and moving to Celestial Falls." My mate's hand jerks in my hold, but I give her a squeeze and continue. "We will raise our family here." That should put some of his concerns to rest.

"Is the war council aware of your intentions?" I guess Aurora's father isn't ready to blindly trust me.

"They are." I explain, "I've been training my replacement."

"Why the fuck did you fight tooth and nail to get that position if you didn't plan to keep it?" It's the same question my immediate supervisor had when I submitted my retirement plans.

"I wanted to prove myself worthy of my mate." I stare into his eyes, hoping he sees my sincerity.

That takes the wind out of the asshole's sails. Cupid runs his hand down his face and swallows. "Well, fucking hell."

"Now apologize." Layla Amor pokes her finger into his chest.

"I'm sorry I didn't kick your ass years ago before you got your hooks into my daughter," he snarls, earning a glare from his wife.

Knowing I need to play nice with the future outlaws, I invite them to stay for brunch. It ends up being the most uncomfortable two hours I've ever spent in my life. Attempting to consume human food while the God of Love glares at you turns my stomach. By the time we walk the Amors to the door, I've had my limit for the day.

"Thank you for trying so hard to reassure my dad." Aurora wraps her silky arms around my waist and leans up to kiss my chin. "Don't worry. The big lug will come around."

I'm not so sure, but I don't argue with my love.

That night, I lay in the dark with Aurora curled up next to me making plans. Thankfully, my fae blood allows me to survive on very little sleep.

My little mate doesn't argue when I convince her to move in permanently. When she introduces me to her older brother, I discover friendship. Over the next few weeks, I manage to cut back my hours at the war council to spend more time with my girl.

August teaches me to play video games, and I develop a whole new obsession. Before long, my mate's brother spends several afternoons a week at the penthouse playing games with me. It's a welcome distraction while I adjust to life on the outside.

"You sound like you've been in prison." Aurora sits next to me on the sofa. I felt her slipping into my consciousness earlier but didn't stop her entry. I have nothing to hide from my little love.

"Being away from you is like prison." I hug her luscious curves tight.

"You're such a suck-up," she teases before squealing when I throw her over my shoulder.

"I'll show you sucking up. And down." I smack her curvy ass and feel a tremor run through her body. My little love likes a good spanking every now and then.

CHAPTER 9

AURORA

Over the next few months, we finish up the renovations on the penthouse, and Nix officially retires from the war council. Our life settles into a fairly normal pattern. Well, mostly normal. My dad still gives Nix hell any chance he gets, but my fae hottie takes it in stride. Hopefully, my father will reconsider when he finds out we're going to have a little fae munchkin soon.

When I started feeling a little off a few weeks ago, I thought it was the stress of moving and settling into my new home that was to blame for the ailment. Before long, other signs popped up. When the smell of fish sent me rushing to the bathroom, I couldn't deny it any longer. Our frequent "mating" had produced lifelong results, too.

Nix taught me to keep certain thoughts private, and I'm using my new skill to hide this from my mate. Not for long, but until I have time to find the right way to tell him.

Luckily, I have tons of other things keeping my poor mind occupied. We moved Design Goddesses into the extra study. I had planned to put my little cottage on the market, but my brother decided to buy it from me. August doesn't share our father's reservations about Nix. Matter of fact, the two men became best friends almost instantly. I'm getting tired of my brother coming over to play video games with my mate daily.

Once I finish up for the day, I head to the den and find Nix and August glued to the screen, fighting an imaginary war. "You should leave before traffic gets bad." I don't care if it's rude. I haven't seen my husband since lunchtime, and I'm missing his touch.

"I guess that's my sign to leave." August stands up and stretches. "You want to pick this up again tomorrow?" He glances over at Nix.

"I can't." My mate refuses before I'm able to put my foot down. "I'm taking my little love away for the weekend." That's news to me.

"Well, I'll see you Monday then." August isn't fazed. He gives me a little peck on the cheek and heads out.

"When did you plan on telling me about our," I emphasize *our*, "plans?"

"I planned to fuck you until you couldn't stand, then inform you, but your bonehead brother changed my plans."

"You know you love my bonehead brother." I wrap my arms around his waist before glancing up to wiggle my eyebrows. "I have a great idea. Why don't I act like I know nothing, and you can carry out your plan?"

I squeal as my mate throws me over his shoulder and races for the bedroom. His warm palm comes down hard on my backside a few times, and the quick smacks cause tiny bites of pleasure-pain to shoot straight to my pussy.

My laughter turns to groans as he uses his magic to rip our clothes away. I'll never complain about that little trick. "You're soaking wet." He slips his finger between my legs and traces my intimate lips. "I should probably do something about that."

Nix sets me on the brand-new leather sofa in our reading nook and drops between my spread thighs. "I need to taste you." He tugs my hips to the edge and leans down to devour the wetness dripping from my center.

My knees shake as ecstasy overtakes me. He slides two fingers into my pussy and runs them around my sensitive inner walls. His pleasure mixes with mine in our combined thoughts and the sensations amplify. When he gently bites down on my clit, and whispers, "Come," in my mind, I follow his orders.

When the lights finally quit dancing behind my closed eyelids, I find myself laying in our bed. "Nice of you to return to me." Nix kisses his way up my chest, stopping to suck on each of my nipples. Another climax tingles at the base of my spine, but I hold it back, wanting to enjoy my mate.

"Now, I'm going to fuck you bowlegged." I roll my eyes. His English accent pronouncing *bowlegged* makes me giggle.

My giggle turns into a moan as he presses his huge erection into my wet center. "Fuck me." His heated growl tells me that my mate enjoys my dirty mouth.

His pounding thrusts nail me to the bed as I hold on to his shoulders to keep from slamming my head into our new ornate headboard. All too soon, the tingling moves from my toes straight up my legs, and I realize I'm going to come. I pull his head down and close my teeth over the vein pulsing in his neck, sending my mate over the edge with me.

Nix drops to his back and pulls me close. "I think my little goddess has some cougar floating around in there." He smirks down at me.

"My mother would be happy to hear that. She's always sworn both of us kids take after my dad."

"Please, don't bring up your parents while my cock is still pulsing from tearing up your pussy." He fake shudders. "It messes with my performance."

"Believe me. There is nothing wrong with your performance. If you performed any better, I'd walk with a permanent limp."

"It's a goal." Nix kisses the side of my neck before showing me how he works toward his goals.

CHAPTER 10

AURORA

The next day, we leave for our weekend trip. When Nix refuses to tell me where we're going, I try to find out by using the old "I need to know what to bring" excuse.

My mate sees through my attempt and responds, "You'll be naked the whole time so don't bring anything."

I end up packing for just about anything. "I told you not to bring a lot." Nix frowns when he sees my three suitcases sitting at the back door. "That won't fit into my trunk."

In the end, I leave one of the bags after Nix tells me we're going to Blaze's hunting cabin. His dragon stepbrother's getaway in the woods sits on thirty acres of private land that borders Firestone Manor, the estate where Nix's father and stepmother live. With the dense forest on one side, the family manor on the other, and a tree-lined pond making up the back of the property, we'll have complete privacy at the dragon's hideaway.

When we arrive, Nix takes me on a tour of the large open cabin. My inner interior designer drools over the beautifully decorated sunken living room with two massive leather sectionals. "Blaze and Anastasia, his mate, have a fucking huge brood," Nix explains. "They reproduce like rabbits." A little bit of fear cuts through me at the thought of my mate not wanting our offspring. Brushing away the worry, I tell myself to relax and enjoy the weekend.

After unpacking, Nix grills steaks on the back patio while I make baked potatoes and salad in the state-of-the-art kitchen. We finish up and clean the kitchen together before heading into the living room to watch a movie on the wall-sized flat screen.

Nix chooses a sappy romantic comedy, which makes me laugh. "Are you feeling like a little romance?" I tease my fae hottie.

"Well, since you asked." My heart freezes in my chest when he slips off the sofa and kneels at my feet. "I'm hoping you'll let me romance you for the rest of eternity." He holds up a tiny blue box for me to see the huge diamond ring sitting in the velvet interior. "I realize this is a silly human tradition, but I want everyone in the universe to know you're mine."

"You want a human wedding?" I must make sure we're on the same page.

"I need to fully mate you. In the eyes of the gods, humans, and shifters, I want everyone to know you belong to me for all eternity. The two of us forever." He slides the ring on my finger before leaning down to place a kiss across my knuckles. "I don't necessarily need the whole crazy human wedding thingy." On that, we both agree.

"There's something you need to know." I can't keep my secret anymore. "Just so you know, it's not going to be only the two of us for very long."

Nix misunderstands my meaning and rushes to reassure me, "I don't care if I have to put up with your asshole father. Having you is worth the small sacrifice."

"That's not exactly what I meant." I open the tiny trap door in my brain and let my secret flow between us.

"Holy shit." A huge smile breaks out on Nix's face. "A mini-god or goddess running around." He lays his head in my lap and slides his hand softly up and down my tummy. "I'll have back up to help me torture your dad."

"Oh no, mister." I push him back onto the real sheep rug in front of the fireplace. "You won't use our children to torture my father."

"Oh, please," he begs and snaps his fingers, removing all our clothes. "You can't take that away from me."

"Maybe you can use your big magic wand to change my mind." I crawl over his body and sink down on his hard cock. As his erection fills me to the brim, I slowly rotate my hips.

My mate's eyes roll back in his head as he whispers, "Anything for you, love."

Nix places his huge palms on my hips and uses his hold to pull me down to meet his fast upward thrusts. "Play with your tits," he groans, and I reach up to wrap my fingers around my nipples. As I pluck the sensitive buds, he slips his thumb between us to rub my clit. Sparks shoot from the tip of my toes all the way to every nerve in my body. I grind my pussy hard against his massive erection, trying to catch the climax hovering right out of my reach. When Nix leans up and sucks my nipple into his mouth, I shudder. He bites down gently, and the orgasm blasts through me.

I flop down onto his chest while his cock finishes jerking deep inside me.

"I love you." I run my fingers over his nearly hair-less chest and sigh.

"I love you, too." He reaches between us to caress my stomach. "And I love this little guy so much. I feel like my heart is going to burst from all this happiness."

"Life is good," I agree and enjoy the feel of his muscular body surrounding mine.

EPILOGUE - NIX

Before we return to Celestial Falls, Blaze's judge friend agrees to marry us. My father, stepmother, and stepbrother are our only witnesses as the human judge joins us in the eyes of the human law.

After a quick lunch, I load up the car and take my family home. "I'm sure quietly getting married will give your father another reason to hate me." I glance over at my wife, my mate, my everything.

"You're wrong. He's going to think you're the best thing since sliced bread." Aurora pats her stomach softly. "Now, he might freak a little when he remembers how babies are made."

That's an understatement. The earth shakes when my father-in-law roars his displeasure at me "knocking up" his baby girl.

Luckily, his anger lessens over my mate's pregnancy. By the time our tiny daughter makes her entrance three weeks early, Val is over the moon for his first grandchild. Actually, the entire family embraces our newest addition.

The day we get home from the hospital, the whole family ascends on our new house. Once I discovered my mate's little secret, I knew there was no way I would raise my kids in a penthouse. I found us the perfect home halfway between Firestone Manor and my outlaw's home. Sometimes, I wonder if it's too close to our crazy relatives.

"You have to stop calling my parents your outlaws," my wife hisses at me mentally, and I glance over at her and wink. Dark circles surround her stunning green eyes, and she hasn't put any effort into her appearance, but she's still the most beautiful creature I've ever seen.

"Not any time soon." I smirk at my mate before turning to watch Layla snuggle our newborn daughter close.

"She looks just like you," Layla tells my mate. "So freaking adorable."

"All this gushiness and love is turning my stomach," my brother-in-law cuts in.

When August rolls his eyes and starts making gagging noises, Blaze shakes his head and warns him, "I wouldn't do that. You're daring the Fates to make you eat those words. I mean, if the old broads can find someone to put up with this asshole," he points at me, and I mentally flip off the fucker, "you're in real trouble."

Both Val and Layla groan when their son shrugs. "I'm not worried. Let them do their worst."

When my infant daughter starts fussing, I push my brother-in-law's idiotic dare to the back of my mind and jump in to take my little girl from her grandmother. "I'm going to check her diaper," I tell them and take Lydia up to her room. "Come meet me. Act like you're making sure everything is okay." I send a mental message to my wife.

"You're using our child to get away from our families." Aurora steps into the nursery and closes the door. "I love the way you think." She reaches for Lydia. "Plus, I think the little goddess would like some dinner."

I sit on the window seat and watch my wife feed our baby. "Can I have a little taste when she's done?" I ask my mate, only half-joking. Her luscious swollen tits call to me.

"When my girly parts finish healing, you can taste all you want." She shakes her head. "Until then, keep your magic wand under control and away from me."

"I can live with that." I walk over and run my finger down the sleeping infant's cheek. "Thank you for giving me the world." I stare into her eyes and let her feel all the happiness and contentment running through my soul.

"I love you." I see tears form in her emerald green eyes and wonder how long the crazy pregnancy hormones will continue to affect her. The crying at the drop of a hat gets old, but the intense sexual appetite is pretty amazing. Maybe I should just knock her up again.

"Oh, heck no." Aurora shakes her head. "I'm not doing this again any time soon."

My mate ends up eating her words. Spectacularly. I finally give her a break six years later after our fifth daughter is born. Life couldn't get any better. Every day, I make sure to thank the three crabby Fates for bringing my curvy goddess into my life.

THE END OF *Aurora's Fae Prince*

JOIN MY READER'S GROUP

FIND OUT ABOUT MY NEW RELEASES, SALES AND OTHER PROMOTIONS.

Facebook Group (Hot Heroes and Happy Endings)

SUBSCRIBE TO MY NEWSLETTER

GET HOW TO LOVE A HEARTBREAKER WHEN YOU SUBSCRIBE TO MY NEWSLETTER

Loni Ree Romance Newsletter

ALSO BY LONI REE

Find all my books on my website:

https://www.hotheroesandhea.com/

SILVER SPOON MC

The CEO

The Cowboy

The Rockstar

The Architect

The Prince

SILVER SPOON FALLS

Fischer's Catch

Adam's Fugitive

MONSTERS & CURVES

Mr. Nice Guy

First Bite

CELESTIAL FALLS

Cupcakes & Brimstone

Honey & Growls

Hexes & Howls

Whiskers & Wings

Glitz & Growls

Defying Roderick (Related to Celestial Falls)

CURVY CUTIES

Jenna

Emery

BOSS FROM HELL

Over It

Into It

WILD ACES

Spade's Queen

Barrett's Play

Snow's Spell (connected characters)

MEN OF VALOR MC

First Ride

FIELDING-STONE SERIES

Blindsiding Mr. Quinlan

Shocking Mr. Stone

Fielding-Stone Series Boxset

Candy Kisses

Kane's Kisses: A Four Book Collection Boxset

Forever Kisses

SWEET BEGINNINGS

Sweet Treat

Sugar Pie

LOVING A BENNETT BOY

Mr. CEO Jerk

Mr. Director Sir

Mr. Boss Man

SPARKS IN JUNIPER

Ignite My Heart

FINDING MS. RIGHT

Claiming Ms. Off Limits

Roping Ms. Imposter

PLAYING RIORDAN

Catching Payton

Scoring Gina

FALLING HARD AND FAST

Can't Resist Her

THE MERGER

Blake's Fall

Lukas' Love

Drew's Fight

FIRSTS SERIES

First Sight

First Touch

SWEET ON YOU (CLEAN, SWEET ROMANCE) Writing
as L. Ree

Knox's Surprise (Sweet on You Book 1)

Trace's Fire (Sweet on You Book 2)

Jordan's Gift (Sweet on You Book 3)

Jason's Luck (Sweet on You Book 4)

ABOUT THE AUTHOR

USA Today Bestselling Author

Loni Ree is a very busy mom of six who loves to read, and she finds that it helps her escape the chaos of everyday life. She likes quick reads that are red-hot and on the excessive side. Writing has also been a passion of hers, and Loni decided to share the stories floating around in her mind. Her short, steamy stories are a little over the top because she believes reading should be an escape from real life. She writes about hot heroes finding their beautiful soulmates and fighting for their happy endings!

Loni also has an alternate pen name L. Ree. If you like clean, sweet romance, check out her L. Ree books.

Website: Hotheroesandhea.com
https://linktr.ee/loniree19

facebook.com/lonireeromance

twitter.com/loni_ree

instagram.com/lonireeromance

amazon.com/author/loniree

bookbub.com/authors/loni-ree

goodreads.com/LoniRee

pinterest.com/loni01013104